A SCARF FOR KEIKO

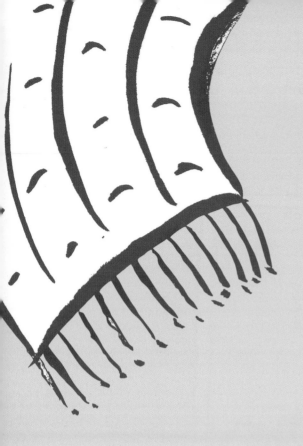

DEDICATED TO THE MEMORY OF CHARLENE ETSUKO UNOKI
—A.M.

FOR A., O., AND M. MAY YOU REMEMBER TO SHARE
KINDNESS AND LOVE ALWAYS.
—M.L.

Acknowledgments

In writing this story, I relied heavily on the Japanese American National Museum's book *Los Angeles's Boyle Heights*, Elizabeth Fine Ginsburg's essay "Students were Stunned at the Sudden Disappearance of our Japanese Classmates" in *Western States Jewish History*, and the Japanese American internment photographs of Ansel Adams and Dorothea Lange. Special thanks to Bill Watanabe and the Little Tokyo Historical Society, Steve Crise, my editor Amy Fitzgerald, and my fellow writers Linda Asako Angst, Joan Axelrod-Contrada, Linda Salzman Cohen, Kathy Cowie, Mary Ann Castronovo Fusco, Alan Grossman, Susan Keeter, and Liz Rice.

KAR-BEN PUBLISHING, INC.
A division of Lerner Publishing Group, Inc.
241 First Avenue North
Minneapolis, MN 55401 USA
1-800-4-KARBEN

Website address: www.karben.com

Photographs on pages 30 and 31 are courtesy of the National Archives and Library of Congress.

Main body text set in Johnson ITC Std Medium 14/20.
Typeface provided by International Typeface Corp.

Library of Congress Cataloging-in-Publication Data

Names: Malaspina, Ann, author. | Liddiard, Merrilee, illustrator.
Title: A scarf for Keiko / by Ann Malaspina ; illustrated by Merrilee Liddiard.
Description: Minneapolis : Kar-Ben Publishing, [2019] | Series: [Kar-Ben favorites] | Summary: In Little Tokyo, Los Angeles, in 1942, after Sam's Japanese neighbor, Keiko, is sent to an internment camp with her family, he makes a special effort to send her a gesture of friendship.
Identifiers: LCCN 2018011904 (print) | LCCN 2018018417 (ebook) | ISBN 9781541542181 (eb pdf) | ISBN 9781541521643 (lb : alk. paper) | ISBN 9781541521650 (pb : alk. paper)
Subjects: LCSH: World War, 1939–1945—United States—Juvenile fiction. | CYAC: World War, 1939–1945—United States—Fiction. | Friendship—Fiction. | Japanese Americans—Fiction. | Jews—United States—Fiction. | Knitting—Fiction. | World War, 1939–1945—United States—Fiction. | Los Angeles (Calif.)—History—20th century—Fiction.
Classification: LCC PZ7.M28955 (ebook) | LCC PZ7.M28955 Sc 2019 (print) | DDC [E]—dc23

LC record available at https://lccn.loc.gov/2018011904

Manufactured in the United States of America
1-44390-34651-7/3/2018

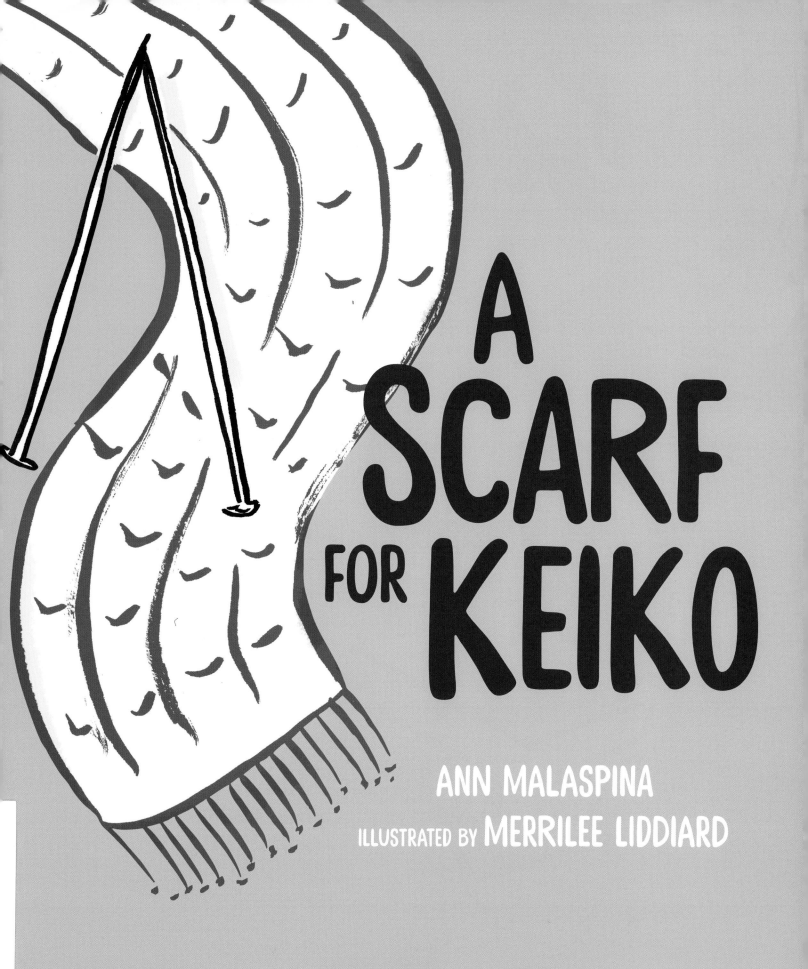

A SCARF FOR KEIKO

ANN MALASPINA

ILLUSTRATED BY MERRILEE LIDDIARD

KAR-BEN
PUBLISHING

THE NEEDLES slipped from Sam's hands, and the wool tangled up in knots. Knitting made him want to pull out his hair.

Next to him, Keiko bent over her wool. Her needles flew like the wind. *Click. Clack. Click. Clack.* Rows of blue stitches grew inch by inch.

"Good work, Keiko," said their teacher, Mrs. Olson. "Having a problem, Sam?"
Click. Clack. Click. Clack.

"Remember, pick up the yarn. Wrap it around the needle. Pull the stitch through," she said. "We must do our part for the war effort. Our soldiers are counting on you, Sam."

That's a mistake! Sam thought. *I'm a terrible knitter. No one should count on me.*

In the lunchroom, Sam felt a tap on his shoulder. Keiko smiled at him. "I can help you with your knitting."

Keiko was Sam's next-door neighbor. Ever since President Roosevelt had declared war on Japan in December, some of Sam's friends refused to talk to Keiko and the other Japanese American students at First Street School in Boyle Heights.

"I don't need any help," mumbled Sam, turning away.

Keiko's smile disappeared. "Suit yourself."

She turned her back and sat at an empty table.

After lunch, Sam played catch with his best friend Jack.

"Have you heard from Mike?" Jack asked as he caught the ball smoothly.

Sam shook his head. When he thought about his older brother fighting in the war, Sam's stomach tied up in knots like the yarn on his desk.

"Don't worry," Jack said. "He's probably too busy winning the war to write a letter."

After school, Sam saw Keiko pedaling past him down East First Street on her fire-engine red bicycle.

A car slowed down. A teenage boy leaned out the window.

Splat! An egg landed on the sidewalk. "Go back to Japan!" the boy yelled.

Her bike skidded, but Keiko didn't fall. She pedaled even faster around the corner as Sam watched.

That night, Sam listened to the radio with his parents. President Roosevelt was announcing the latest war news.

"Do you think we're going to win?" Sam asked.

"If we all do our part," Dad said. "I hear that you're knitting for the soldiers. Good for you!"

Knitting again. Sam sighed.

On the way to school, Keiko's brakes screeched at the crosswalk.

"Hello, Sam." Knitting needles stuck out of her bag.

Standing next to Jack, Sam pretended not to hear.

"How's Mike?"

The light changed and they pushed across the street.

"I hope he's okay!" Keiko shouted, flying down the street.

Jack elbowed him. "You shouldn't talk to Keiko Saito. What would Mike think?"

Sam's brother had helped Keiko fix her bicycle once. He had shown her how to patch a flat tire and grease the chain. Mike wouldn't mind Sam talking to Keiko. But that was too hard to explain to Jack.

"I didn't talk to her," Sam said. "She talked to me."

On Friday, Mom asked Sam to go to her favorite flower shop in Little Tokyo to pick up flowers for the Shabbat table.

The trolley stopped in front of Mr. Saito's grocery store. Mr. Saito was sweeping up broken glass.

Sam got off the trolley, with his head down. Mr. Saito didn't see him.

The flower shop was closed.

Just before sunset, Mom lit the Shabbat candles
and said the blessing. After they sat down, Dad said the
blessings over the wine and the challah.

As they began to eat, Dad cleared his throat.

"President Roosevelt is worried that people with Japanese ancestors are spies," he said. "He's sending them away."

Mom shook her head. "The war is terrible. My sisters in Poland are in great danger. Mike is risking his life to fight. And now Little Tokyo looks like a ghost town."

Sam put down his fork. "But Keiko isn't a spy!"

"Of course she isn't," Dad said.

Mom nodded. "I'm going to invite the Saitos for dinner tomorrow. They're good Americans, and the best neighbors."

Keiko wasn't at school on Monday.
Knitting was a disaster. Sam almost
poked himself in the eye.

He threw down his needles. "I can't do it!"

Mrs. Olson said he could write a letter to Mike instead.

After school, Keiko was sitting on her front steps.

"Hello, Keiko!" Sam called out.

She didn't look up. The only sound was her needles.

Click. Clack. Click. Clack.

"The Saitos can't come to dinner," Mom told Sam. "They have to pack. They just learned they're being sent north to an internment camp in the desert."

She gestured at the unfamiliar tea set on the kitchen table. "They can only bring what they can carry, so I offered to take care of Mrs. Saito's precious tea set. I told her it will be here when they get home."

"How long will they be away?" Sam asked.

Mom sighed. "No one knows."

And then they were gone.

The morning after the
Saitos left, Sam saw it: Keiko's
bicycle in front of his house.
On the handlebars was a pair
of blue wool socks with a note.

Sam shivered. The desert where Keiko was going
would be cold at night.

In his mother's yarn bag, Sam found a ball of
red wool. Socks were too hard to make, but Sam
could knit something else for Keiko.

He remembered Mrs. Olson's advice:
Pick up the yarn.
Wrap it around the needle.
Pull the stitch through.

Click. Clack. Click. Clack.

Come home safely, Mike and Keiko.

Click. Clack. Click. Clack.

Come home safely.

Sam's needles flew faster and faster—and rows of red stitches grew inch by inch.

AUTHOR'S NOTE

This story takes place in the Los Angeles neighborhoods of Boyle Heights and nearby Little Tokyo, where Jews and Japanese Americans lived side by side and attended schools together in the early decades of the 20th Century.

When Japanese planes bombed the U.S. naval base at Pearl Harbor on December 6, 1941, President Franklin D. Roosevelt declared war on Japan. Even though they had done nothing wrong, suspicion fell on Japanese Americans, and their patriotism and loyalty were questioned. A few months later the President signed Executive Order 9066 authorizing the removal of Japanese Americans to internment camps. The Order was aimed at all people of Japanese descent living near the Pacific Ocean, including American citizens born in the United States, like Keiko in this story.

When copies of this Order appeared on telephone poles and storefronts, many Japanese Americans had to close their businesses and pack their possessions. Men, women, and children lined up to board buses, trucks, cars, and trains for the trips to the camps. Wearing a tag stamped with a number that identified their family, they could bring only what they could carry.

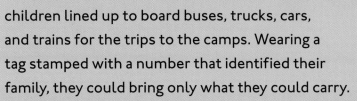

Top: *Example of Civilian Exclusion Order directing removal of persons of Japanese ancestry from a California city.*

Left: *Following evacuation orders, this store was closed. The owner, of Japanese descent, placed the "I AM AN AMERICAN" sign on the storefront the day after Pearl Harbor.*

Left: Members of the Mochida family awaiting evacuation. Mr. Mochida operated a nursery and greenhouses where he raised snapdragons and sweet peas.

Bottom: Evacuees of Japanese ancestry boarding trains for internment camp in Manzanar, California.

4-1-42. Los Angeles - Japanese leaving

Families were taken to ten isolated camps, where they were crowded into barracks behind barbed-wire fences. Guards kept watch from towers.

The internment camps closed only after the war ended in 1945. Many people had lost their homes, job, and possessions. They had to rebuild their lives from scratch.

President Ronald Reagan eventually signed the Civil Liberties Act of 1988, which required the government to pay each survivor of the camps $20,000 and to set up a $1.25 billion education fund for their descendants. The act included an apology to the Japanese American community and acknowledged that "a grave injustice had been done."

Born in Brooklyn, New York, **ANN MALASPINA** has written over 30 books for young people. She has an M.F.A. in Writing for Children and Young Adults from Vermont College of Fine Arts. Her books are about civil rights, literacy, nature, and people who faced great obstacles. She writes under a skylight in northern New Jersey.

MERRILEE LIDDIARD grew up in a home filled with delightful artistic chaos and ample creativity. She spent most of her youth making things out of oatmeal boxes and drawing little humans or animals, and telling the tales that went along with them. She is known for her love of kids' art design, toys and DIY crafts. When not drawing or creating things for her three children, Merrilee loves to travel, wander museums, sew, thrift, read and nap.